T0113569

NOCTURNAL CONSCIOUS

by SD Shock

ARCHWAY
PUBLISHING

To my girls

———◦◦◦———

Everyone is going through something.

Happiness is hard to find and even
harder to hold on to, so never miss
a chance to grab it whether it's
one second, one minute, one hour,
one day, one week, one month,
or one year, and never be sad that
it is gone. Be grateful that it happened.
A small amount of happiness
can erase so much pain.

- SD Shock

———◦◦◦———

Archway Publishing books may be ordered through booksellers or by contacting:

Archway Publishing
1663 Liberty Drive
Bloomington, IN 47403
www.archwaypublishing.com
844-669-3957

Because of the dynamic nature of the Internet, any web addresses or
links contained in this book may have changed since publication and
may no longer be valid. The views expressed in this work are solely those
of the author and do not necessarily reflect the views of the publisher,
and the publisher hereby disclaims any responsibility for them.

ISBN: 978-1-6657-4101-9 (sc)
ISBN: 978-1-6657-4100-2 (e)

Library of Congress Control Number: 2023905692

Print information available on the last page.

Archway Publishing rev. date: 03/22/2023

NOCTURNAL CONSCIOUS

by SD Shock

1

What do you do when the government
        divides you?
Stand in line with your hand out,
Begging on your knees like a dog
        for the scraps they left out.

Teaching you to hate everyone
        that's done better than you.
Jealous and mad 'cause you feel left out.
Scared to enter the race
        'cause you started in last place.

Worshiping celebrities on your hands
        and knees with your tongue out
But hate the man that works hard
        every day to earn his pay
and refuses to believe and give up
        on the dream he creates.

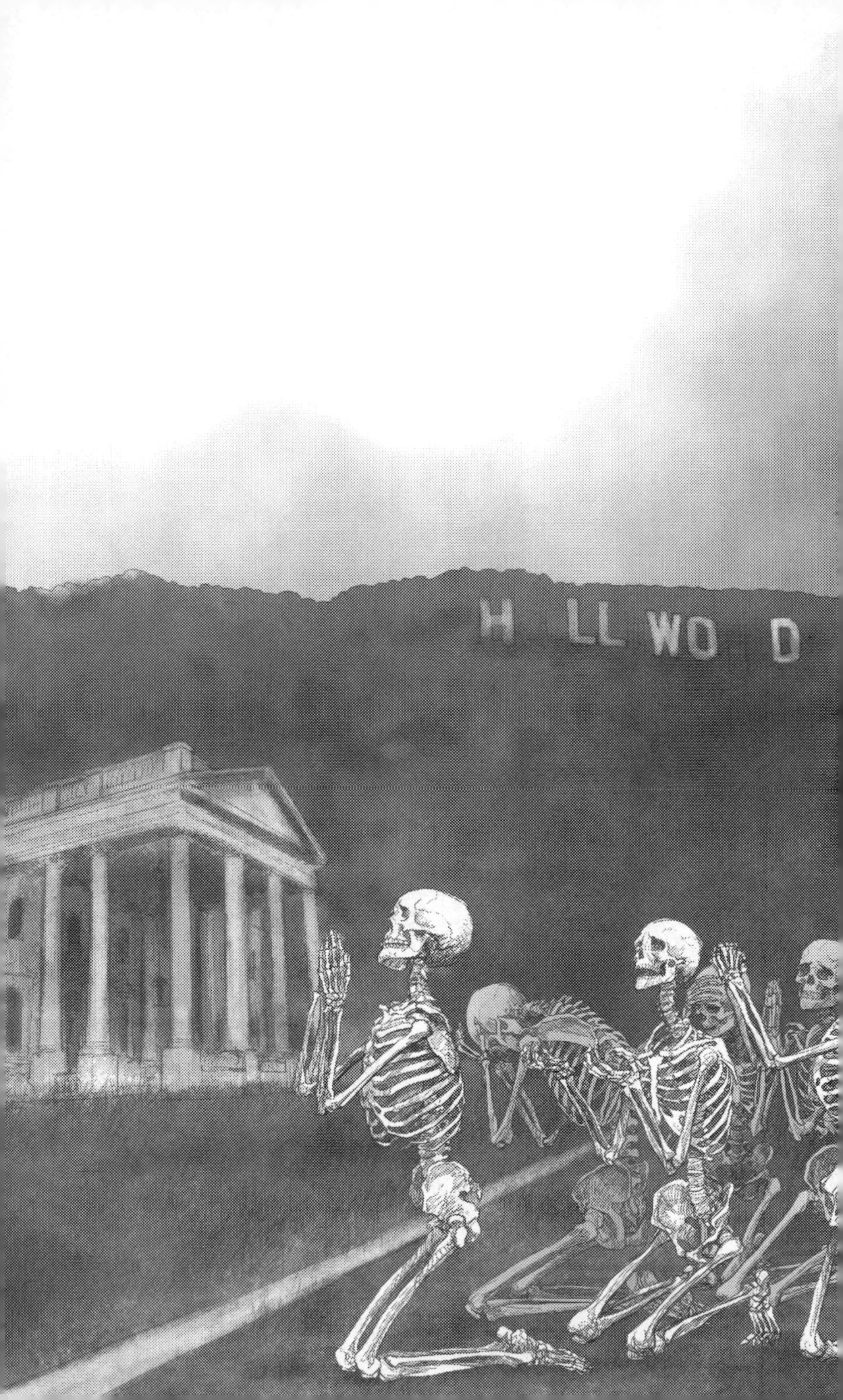
H LLWO D

2

I am not Superman anymore.
     Depression, hate, and suicidal
     thoughts stripped my cape.

The superhero is out. I moved on with
     no compassion or love,
     superpowers all gone.
I am not helpful now that I am weak,
reaching out with no hand for me to take,
screaming at the top of my lungs,
     hoping for help that will never come.

We learn some tough lessons
     as we get old.
     People we thought were friends
will turn their backs and leave you
     out in the cold.

I am the villain who went from lying
      on my couch chilling
at seventeen and eighteen out here,
      killing.

I wish I could turn my brain off.
Can you give me some more of
      those meds, doc?

What happens when I feel the need
      to take a life 'cause they cut me off
      at that traffic light?
And they sent me to counseling?
It doesn't work anymore.

The madman flipped the switch and
kicked down the door.

What happens when the machine
      you built doesn't care anymore
and craves killing worse than before?

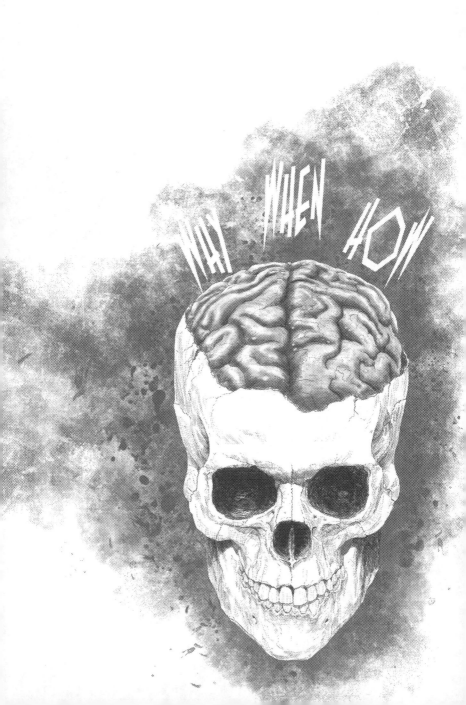

Time is not on your side; you know
        you're going to die.
You don't even get to choose the how or
the why; even suicide is a mystery.

Nobody knows why the brain gets messed
        up and you take your own life.
I don't believe there was a plan...
        had the gun in your hand, removed
        the brain, removed the pain.
I guess not everyone is long for this life.

For the short time you were here,
        you shined.
No one around, you hid the signs.
You seemed happy to them.

We're left with the why

AND

What we could have done.
At the end of it all, it was your time.
No, when or why, just gone.

How much is peace worth?
What if you could live your life with
        no more trauma, no more drama?
What if you could wipe the pain away like
        brush strokes on a painting like
        only Vincent van Gogh could paint?
It's possible if you come to a place
        where your mind is awake.

Turn off the TV.
You can't imagine what a difference
        it makes.
They own your head.
They own your mind and won't be happy
        till big corporations get every dime.

Open your eyes and awaken your mind.
You may find peace and won't lose
        your mind.

We live in a country that will spend
        billions on war,
but not one cent on the poor.
Have you ever opened your eyes and
        wondered why the politicians get
        rich? Why they expect you to dig
        a ditch for a couple of cents?

A two-party system that doesn't give
        a shit if you starve or die,
Why won't you open your mind?
Are you scared of what you will find?
That you have lived a lie?
Check a box on a form.
Let government decide what line
        to put you in.
the great racial divide.

Free is not free if you know the poor.
We are the ones that fight the rich
        man's war.
White trash or come from the hood,
no one gives a shit; we are all
        misunderstood.

I'm not mad if you think I am.
You don't understand it's the price we pay.
At the fuckin' VA stand in line and
        wait my turn, they
gave me some more pills to feel good.

You're home now, son, you did good.
Put your flag on the lawn.
You should be proud of shooting
        the enemies down.
Why you crying?
We gave you a skill.
You know how to kill.

The hospital told me I going to die
I am only forty-nine.
I wish God or Satan would have taken
      me when I was thirty-six.
Found me shot in the head,
      lying in a ditch.
I would not have felt a thing
It would have taken me real quick.

I'm walking disease the punishment
      I receive for doing my job?
Would I have changed things if I had
      a crystal ball to see what the
      future would hold?
That I would fail at this life? I have lived
      and feel all the pain I have caused.

or

Would I not have changed a thing?
Pulling a trigger will take you far when
      I think about the financial gain,
big houses and fancy cars.
Don't need a college degree to kill.

What's life about?
     Have you figured it out?
It's survival of the fittest.
What if we all dropped out?
Said forget it,
quit our jobs working for the man,
and stopped going to school programmed
     by a system built on bias 100 years
     ago to hold down the poor and
     keep us violent.

Do you understand they will use you up?
You are a pawn in the game,
a piece on the board,
a very small part of the corporate
     machine that will eat you up
and throw you out like garbage
     if you make a fuss.

Will you ever open your eyes
     and get off the bus?
If you don't own the business,
     it doesn't mean much.
When you get old, they suck your soul.
It's off you go to move in with the kids
     or the senior citizen home.

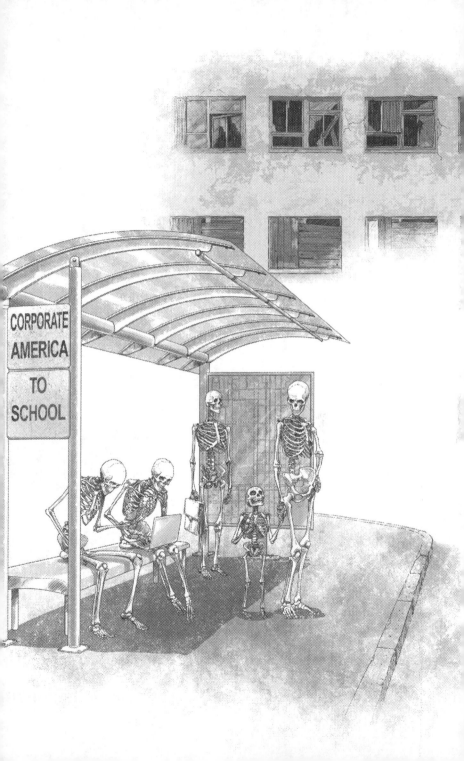

10

I remember the day they called.
The guy on the other end of the phone
said it was an accident gone wrong.
Sorry to tell you, but your brother is gone.
He is dead; someone fucked up.
But they were young, so don't get mad.
It was a kid; your brother seemed old.
   God rest his soul.
He lived a full life.
That's what I was told.

Do you think he was done with
   his time in the sun?
I guess it doesn't matter.
These things just happen.
It's amazing how you handle his loss.
You walked through hell without even
   a thought.
I know you were close,
   but it doesn't matter.
No time to mourn or remember
   your brother.

11

People come into your life
     and then walk away,
taking little pieces with them
     along the way.
Did they come here to teach me a lesson?
What was the lesson that you can make
     me a weapon who hates and
     doesn't love anymore?
Should I be grateful I let these users
     walk through the door and take
     until there is nothing left anymore?
My heart is so cold it can't love anymore.

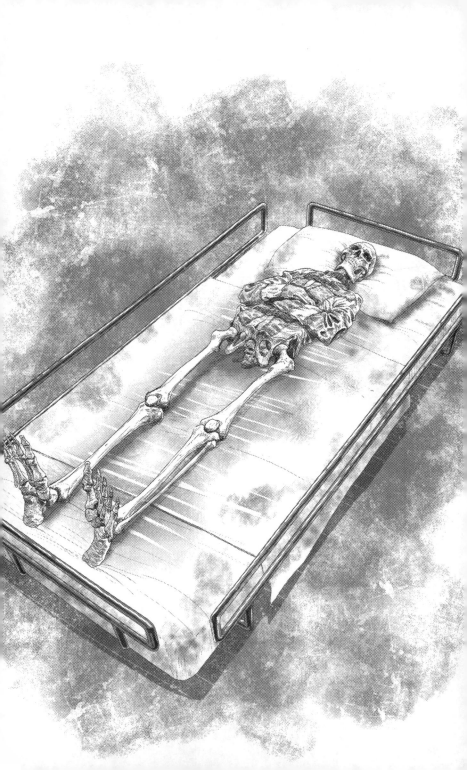

12

Do you know what it's like to wake up
      every day of your life hoping
      one thing in the plan you made
      doesn't change because it might
      make you take your own life?
Stressed so bad you can't open the
      front door.
So scared you feel like you lived in
      Baghdad in 2004.
Staying in your house, peeping out your
      window, more paranoid than before.
Mixing alcohol and drugs, hiding
      underneath the covers, and telling
      the psychiatric ward that the
      boogie man, Freddie, and Michael
      live next door.

If I was gone tomorrow, who would care?
Could not find six people to be my
        knuckle bearer.
Sorry for your loss are the words you
        would hear, but you know deep
        down nobody cares.
Somebody stand up and say don't be sad.
Let's all celebrate a life well had.
What did they know about my life?
Who were they to stand up and talk
        on my behalf?
Did you walk in my shoes?
Do you see the pain I have been through?
So when I am gone, don't be fake.
If you don't love me, then please don't
        show up to celebrate.

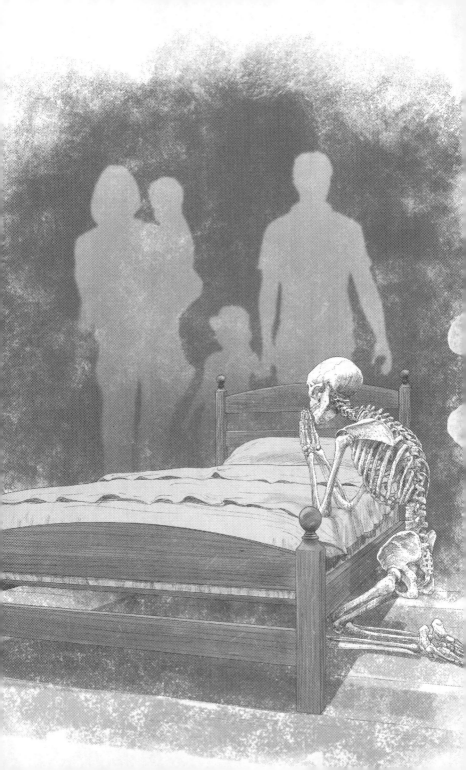

14

Why do you only come to me at night?
    I don't even know your names.
    You know mine. You scream
    about it. I can't stop thinking
    about it.

The medication won't work anymore.
    I don't have anyone else to blame
    anymore. Even the prayers don't
    work anymore.

Was I another paid assassin? They said
    it was a government action, and
    who am I to disagree with the
    political machine? Shut off the
    brain if you want to succeed.
    Am I a tool or machine caught up
    in a world that doesn't agree?

15

Mental illness is a sickness.
     It's trapped in the brain.
It might take a revolver or a doctor
     to remove the pain.
Peace over hate.
I choose to hate.
It's not a debate when you live in a place
     full of ingrates. It's such a disgrace.
Why is it called the human race? I would
     rather sit on the bench and hope
     they all trip and die. They have
     broken my dreams.
I have learned they all lie. Government
     stooges wandering through life and
     don't even know why.
I sit on my bed every day and cry.
The difference between them and me is
     at least I know why.

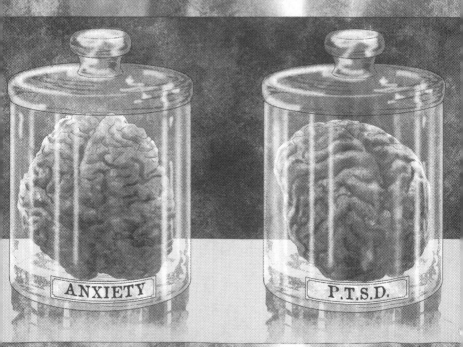

Social media will control your brain,
make you have delusions that only
     cause pain.

Everyone is looking for followers and
     chasing fame
it makes you believe all these
     delusional things
and give you unrealistic hopes and
     false dreams.

Information is good, but what if it's
     not real?
What if it's politicians, corporations,
     and celebrities
undermining your will?

Groupthink manipulation is hard on
     the kids.
Cut back on the technology
and teach them to see things through
     their lens.

17

I hate how life works.
People don't understand.
They will judge you all day for the things
        you have done,
but never once have they given applause
        for what you have overcome.

They don't know and don't care.
All they know is you are guilty,
        and they don't care.
No forgiveness will be given.
No pass will be had.
You are the streets that you come from,
        the family you had.
No exceptions are given; the past
        is not the past.

Accept where you come from
        and stay in your class.
Don't climb up the ladder; we will step
        on those hands.
Stay in your place; we don't care if
        you understand.

People equals hate.
Big crowds make me suffocate.
If I look into your eyes,
you should run and hide.

If you understand you're going to die,
you unleash the monster who is
      bloodthirsty
and wants to kill.
It's me and my delusional mind
that will hunt you down.

Do understand now,
The whole world is full of clowns.
I was built by the government,
so don't fuck around.

So learn my name when I come around.
When you are mentally ill, there are
      triggers all around.
Death awaits when I stare you down.

I don't understand why I only think
    about the life I could have had
    instead of accepting this is all I'm
    ever going to have.

All wrapped up in an unhappy package,
    depressed, broken, and sad.

I reached for the stars and chased the
    dream; it was a nightmare for me.

I was the exception, not the rule.
    I was going to rule the world,
    not end up in pain. Life shattered
    like window panes in an old house
    no one cared about.

Now here I am, hooked on prescription
    drugs, unable to leave my room,
    and scared all the time.
    I'm overthinking my life and the
    things I could have done.

BOOKS BANNED

20

My pain is hidden behind a closed door,
like the chapters of banned books that
      parents won't let their kids read
      anymore.

So did we gain from all the pain I had
      to hide behind those eyes?
Is it worth it now that they can lock you
      down?
It's a republic, right? Or did I
      misunderstand the contract?
Did I read it right?
The man said, "Sign here. You want to
      be a hero, right?"

21

I wish I could heal my pain
instead of seeing a counselor every
        single day.
Get off the meds and
clear my head instead of living in the
clouds through hazed eyes.

It's okay to live a lie and use the
        prescriptions.
It will keep you high.
We all have dealers, even though yours
may look different than mine.

22

If scars or life I have lived an eternity
trapped in my mind,
I can't get out,
I can't escape,
What would you do if you glimpsed
      the world through my eyes?
All the pain, all the hurt, all the death.
Could you survive it?
Or would you be strong enough to
      take your own life?
Or live with the pain?
What would you do if the whole world
      fell on you?
Could you be strong enough to lift it up
      and flip it up,
to keep it from falling on you?

23

Do you know what it's like to be sexually
    assaulted by another man that
    slipped one small pill into your can
    as he stood over you, looking down
    at the strongest man speaking
    those words?
Do you feel powerless now?
How do you feel now lying on the ground
    when I get through with you?
    I bet you never come around.
Do you feel tough now that one little
    pill took you down?
I should kill you, but it's worse to live
    with the disgrace I put you through.
It's written on your face. Now live with
    the shame. I hope you feel the pain.
Your life will never be the same.
        Every time you find happiness,
        I will slip back in your brain.

24

Did you speak up or did you stand in
   silence?
It is on your mind; it weighs on your
   conscience.
Guilt is eating you up now.
Life is not a game that you can press
pause or restart the game.
Choices were made; you live with pain.
Cowards do what cowards do.
      Next time it happens,
      will you stand up or be you?

25

My mind is gone to a wasteland,
and it never returns.
I have tried every treatment,
yet I still mourn the loss of what
will never be.
Monuments erected to all that is lost.
Play "Taps" for it is deceased.
The body is still here.
Will they play the "Star Spangled Banner"
for me?

I didn't die, but I am dead.
I died that day when I failed you.
I passed the day I decided not to go back.
I broke the day I let your family down.
You are dead because of that call.
You needed me, and I said no.
You are no longer here,
but I died that day.

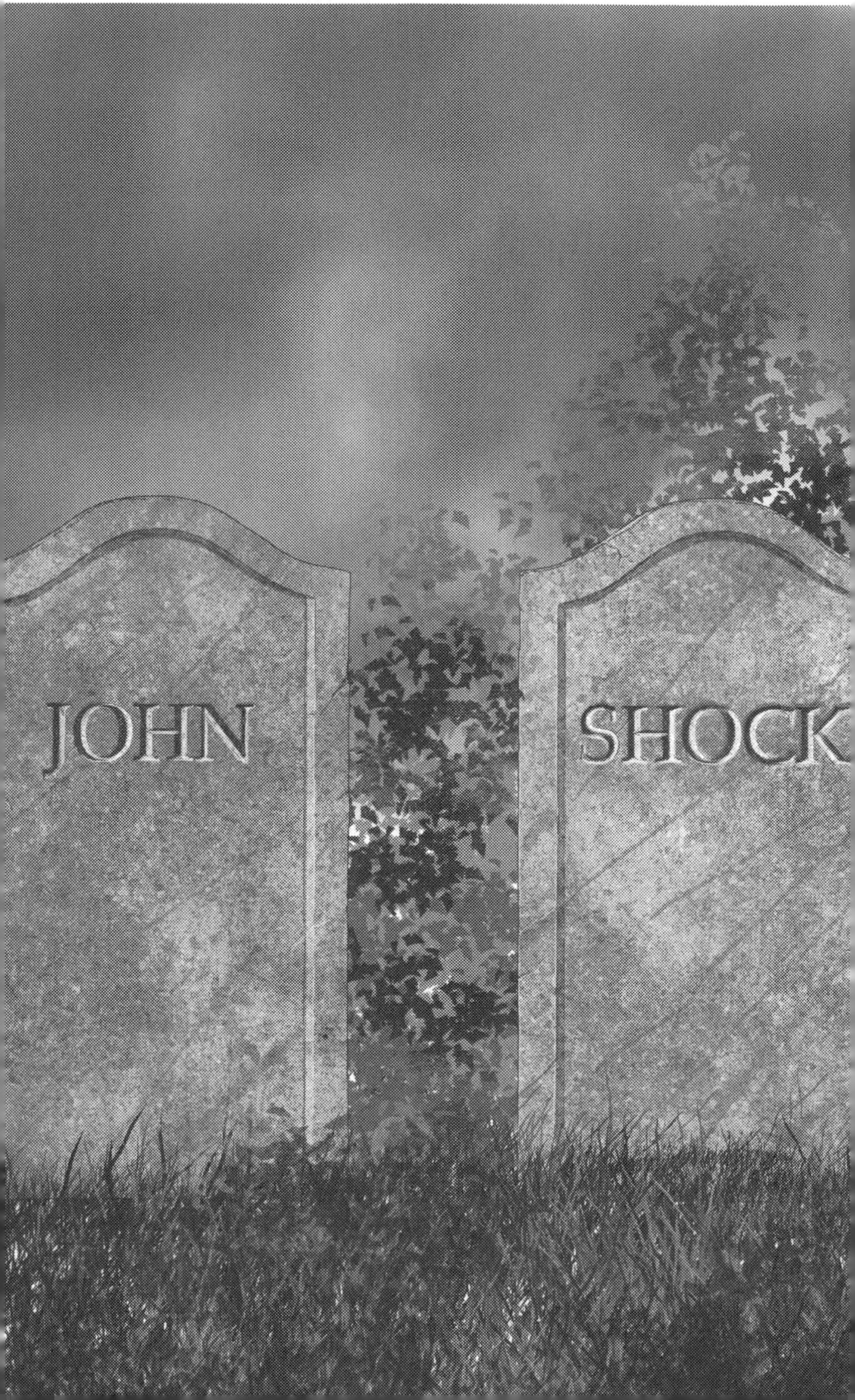
JOHN
SHOCK

Point blank range and I am still here.
Five shots rang out; nobody knew
     I was scared;
     super tough never showed fear.

My reputation was made that day
     eye to eye as we stood in that field.
I never moved and didn't bat an eye.
     I got right real quick;
     I was ready to die.

When the shooting stopped,
     I was still alive.
It made me feel invincible,
     like maybe I couldn't die.
From that day on, my mind got fucked up.
Things got dark. I screamed for help,
     but it didn't come.
I craved cruelty and violence like never
     before. I trained my mind to forget
     compassion and love for war.

I either sleep 20 hours or none at all.
Freddie came to visit my dreams
　　　but got scared and went home.
My nightmares chased him down
　　　the street. He locked himself in a
　　　house, too scared to come out.
The counselor looked inside my head once.
It messed her up so bad she quit her
　　　job the next day.
Now she is a patient at the same VA.

I used to have a beautiful family,
　　　but they moved out, neighbors got
　　　scared, called the cops, thought
　　　I buried them underneath the
　　　house.
Now my yards are all dug up,
　　　and my body's all broke down,
　　　so I can't fix it up.

I was going to pay a man but couldn't
　　　get a loan from the bank because
　　　they didn't think I would be alive
　　　long enough to run the interest up.
It's a beautiful life to be mentally ill
　　　and scary as fuck.

ABOUT THE AUTHOR

SD Shock, a 24-year U.S. Army veteran,
shares his experiences with PTSD,
anxiety, trauma, and suicidal thoughts
while growing up in poverty, as well
as his views on the dysfunctional
political system. His writing represents
the manuscript of life with his
distinctively rhythmic phrases.

Printed in the United States
by Baker & Taylor Publisher Services